Rosie & Jim
at the Seaside

By John Cunliffe Illustrated by Joan and Jane Hickson

A Ragdoll Production for Central Independent Television

Scholastic Children's Books,
Scholastic Publications Ltd,
7-9 Pratt Street, London NW1 0AE

Scholastic Inc.,
730 Broadway, New York, NY 10003, USA

Scholastic Canada Ltd,
123 Newkirk Road, Richmond Hill,
Ontario, Canada L4C 3G5

Ashton Scholastic Pty Ltd,
PO Box 579, Gosford, New South Wales,
Australia

Ashton Scholastic Ltd,
Private Bag 1, Penrose, Auckland,
New Zealand

First published by Scholastic Publications Ltd. 1993

Text copyright © by John Cunliffe 1993
Illustrations copyright © by Joan Hickson 1993

Based on the Central Independent Television
series produced by Ragdoll Productions

ISBN: 0 590 54102 1

Typeset by Rapid Reprographics
Printed in Hong Kong by the Paramount Printing Group

The *Ragdoll* was on her way.
Jim looked out of the hatch.
  "What can you see?" said Rosie.
  "Ermmmmm...a man with a dog,"
said Jim.

3

"Nothing else, noggin?"

"Listen!" said Jim. "Duck's quacking."

"Quick," said Rosie, "follow John."

Rosie and Jim followed John along a grassy path, round by a letter-box, over a sandy hill, and...then they all stopped.

"*Look!*" said Jim.

"Super-fizzy!" said Rosie.

"What is it?" said Jim.

"Greeny-blue stuff."

"Mmmm, the sea, at last," said John.

"It's the sea," said Rosie.

"There's a lot of it," said Jim.

5

Rosie and Jim followed John across the sand.

"It goes all the way," said Rosie, "to the end of the world."

John walked along the beach.

"What a lot of water," said Jim.

"What a lot of people," said Rosie.

John met some friends.

"Fancy meeting you here," they said.

The children were building sand-castles.

"Can I help?" said John.

7

John didn't notice that Rosie and
Jim had joined in. What a
wonderful castle they built! It had
towers, and gates, and rooms, and
a secret tunnel.

It had a moat all round it, and two
canals going all the way across the
sand to the sea. The waves lapped
at the end, and sent little waves
down the canals, making the toy
boats rock to and fro.

John said, "I can't remember
building all that!"

Oh how Rosie and Jim rolled in
the sand, and poked each other,
and laughed! John could never
guess who had built so much of the
castle, but the children knew.

When the sun was low over the sea, the mother said, "Time to go home!"

"Ohhhhh!" said the children.

"But we'll come again tomorrow."

"Hooray!"

"*I'm* not going home," said Rosie.

"What?" said Jim.

"I'm staying here. I'm going to live in this lovely sand-castle."

"But..." said Jim.

"It's much nicer than the poky old *Ragdoll*."

"Oh, but..." said Jim.

"You can go back if you like, I'm staying here, for ever and ever."

"Oh," said Jim. "Then I'll stay with you."

13

Rosie and Jim hid in a room of the sand-castle until everyone had gone. They looked out. It was getting dark. The wide sands were empty now.

"Rosie," said Jim.

"What, noggin?"

"It's...it's...lonely here with no Fizzgog."

"Oh, noggin!"

"And we can't find our way back to the *Ragdoll*."

15

"We don't want to. It's nicer here," said Rosie.

"Is it?"

"Yes, it is," said Rosie. "And we're not going to be silly fizz-pots and feel lonely. We're going to find a nice place to sleep in our lovely new castle."

They crept about in the dark, and found a place to sleep. They made sand-beds for themselves.

"My bed's too hard," said Jim.

"Oh, don't be a soft noggin," said Rosie, "and go to sleep."

Jim tried to sleep, but he could not. There were so many sounds that kept him awake.

They were trickling, and rippling, and running sounds, that came nearer and nearer. The sounds of water, creeping along the sand-canal, and filling the moat deeper and deeper. The sounds of the waves coming closer and closer.

Jim whispered in the dark.

"Rosie? Rosie?"

Rosie sounded cross.

"What is it noggin?"

"Can you hear?"

"What?"

"Listen."

"It's only water. You've heard plenty of that before, on the old *Ragdoll*."

"But the water stays in one place on the canal. It moves about, here."

"Well, pop your head out and have a look."

Jim popped his head out, and
looked over the sand-wall of the
castle. Oh, what a fright he had!
"Rosie! Rosie! It's coming!"
"What's coming, fizz-pot?"

"The sea! It's coming to get us!"

"Rubbish and pipkins! It's a long way away!"

"It *was*, but it isn't now. Look, Rosie, see for yourself!"

Rosie looked out. The sea was
lapping at the walls of the castle.
As they watched, a bigger wave
came, and knocked down all the
front wall. The water flooded in.

"Run!" shouted Rosie.

Rosie and Jim ran. The water
reached across the sand, as though
trying to catch them. They looked
back, and saw a big wave
knocking their sand-castle down.

More waves came and smoothed
the ruins over. Soon, there was
nothing there but smooth sand, and
water that became deeper and
deeper as they watched.

"Oh, Rosie, now we have nowhere to sleep and nowhere to live."

Poor Rosie and Jim, they didn't know what to do. They huddled by a tussock of grass, trying to shelter from the cold sea-wind.

Then they heard a voice.

"Now I wonder if I dropped it here?"

They saw a light.

"Fizzgog!" cried Jim.

"Quiet," said Rosie. "Follow that light."

27

"There it is!" said John. He picked something up and put it in his pocket.

He didn't see that two draggled
ragdolls were following him. He
was in a hurry to get back to his
warm boat. Rosie and Jim *were*
glad to see the *Ragdoll*.

Jim lay awake listening for a long time. He could hear the lapping of canal-water, and the call of an owl.

Perhaps, far away, he might
just be able to hear a whisper
of the sea, but it never came close.
They were safe now. They were
soon asleep.

The next morning Jim looked out of the window to make sure that the sea had not got into the canal. All was well. The water was where it always was.

When Rosie woke up, Jim said, "It's best on the old *Ragdoll*, isn't it, Rosie?"

Rosie just said, "Noggin!" and gave Jim a hug.